Here's the rightful place for my name

THE
LION KING

SCHOLASTIC INC.

New York   Toronto   London   Auckland   Sydney
Mexico City   New Delhi   Hong Kong   Buenos Aires

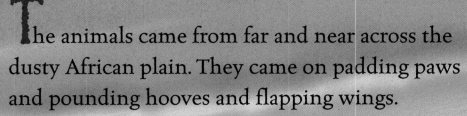

The animals came from far and near across the dusty African plain. They came on padding paws and pounding hooves and flapping wings.

Each beast made its way to Pride Rock. For that was the home of the Lion King, and this was a special day in the Pride Lands.

On this day, Simba,
the first-born cub of
King Mufasa and Queen
Sarabi, would join the
great Circle of Life.

The animals took their places and bowed to King Mufasa.
Then Rafiki, the wise baboon, stood at the edge of Pride
Rock and held up the future lion king for all to see.

A great cry arose from all of the animals.

But one animal did not join in the joyous ceremony.
Scar, the king's jealous brother, stayed in his den.

Later, Scar just laughed when the king's advisor, Zazu the hornbill, criticized him. "As the king's brother, you should have been first in line at Simba's ceremony."

Scar would have eaten Zazu if Mufasa hadn't come along just in time.

Scar's green eyes gleamed. "I was first in line, until the little hairball was born."

"That hairball is my son and your future king," Mufasa growled.

Scar slinked away.

"Don't turn your back on me!" Mufasa warned.

Scar looked back over his shoulder. His eyes narrowed. "Perhaps *you* shouldn't turn your back on *me*."

Simba grew quickly. One morning, Mufasa took his son to the top of Pride Rock and told him, "The Circle of Life never stops turning. One day the sun will set on my time as ruler and rise with you as king. Then everything the light touches will be yours."

"What about the shadowy place?" Simba asked.

Mufasa declared, "You must never go there."

Suddenly Zazu swooped down and squawked, "Hyenas in the Pride Lands!"

Mufasa frowned. "Zazu, take Simba home."

"Aw, Dad, can't I come?" Simba whined.

Mufasa shook his mighty mane. Fighting savage hyenas was no job for a cub.

13

Later, Simba asked Scar about the shadowy place. An evil plan formed in Scar's mind. "Only the bravest lions go to the elephant graveyard," Scar told him. He knew the foolish cub would go there just to prove his bravery.

Scar was right. Simba couldn't wait to go to the elephant graveyard with his best friend, Nala. But how could they go with Zazu watching every move they made?

Soon the two friends found a way to escape their feathered baby-sitter.

Before long, the young lions had reached the dark, mysterious place beyond the borders of the Pride Lands.

"It's kind of scary," Nala whispered.

"Let's check it out," Simba said. "I laugh in the face of danger. Ha-ha-ha!"

"Hee-hee-hee!" cackled three mean hyenas, Shenzi, Banzai, and Ed.

"Look, boys! A king fit for a meal," Shenzi snickered.

The cubs ran but soon found themselves cornered.

Simba stepped
bravely in front of
Nala and tried to roar.
"Rrr . . . rrr."

The hyenas laughed and jeered.
Simba opened his mouth to try again.
This time the ground rattled with a
thunderous *ROAR!*

Mufasa sprang into view and chased away the hyenas.
Zazu had seen the cubs in trouble and flown for help.
Mufasa told Zazu to take Nala home. Then he scolded
Simba for disobeying him.

"I was just trying to be brave, like you," Simba said.

Mufasa sighed. "Being brave doesn't mean you go looking for trouble, Simba. A good king is wise as well as brave."

Simba suddenly felt very small. "We'll always be together. Right, Dad?"

Mufasa looked up at the starry sky and said, "The great kings of the past look down on us from those stars. So whenever you feel alone, just remember that those kings will always be there to guide you . . . and so will I."

Later, Scar met with the hungry hyenas. "I practically gave those cubs to you," he complained.

"They weren't exactly alone," Shenzi whined.

But Scar had another plan that would allow him to become king. "Stick with me, and you'll never go hungry again," he promised.

21

The next morning, Scar took Simba to the bottom of a rocky canyon. "Now wait here," he ordered. "Your father has a big surprise for you."

"Will I like the surprise?" Simba asked.

Scar smiled slyly. "Oh, it's to die for," he said as he walked away. Then he signaled the waiting hyenas.

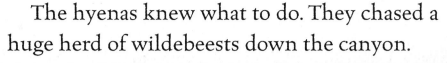

The hyenas knew what to do. They chased a huge herd of wildebeests down the canyon.

Simba felt the earth shake. Then he saw the wildebeests heading straight for him!

Simba managed to climb a dead tree and cling to a branch. "Help!" he shouted.

Meanwhile, Scar had found Mufasa. "Simba's trapped in a stampede!" Scar cried.

Just as Scar had planned, Mufasa rescued Simba,
but then fell under the rushing tide of hooves.

"Dad!" Simba shouted. He couldn't see anything
through the huge dust cloud.

Mufasa tried to pull himself up the steep rocks.
From above, Scar watched his brother struggle.

"Help me! Brother, help me," Mufasa pleaded.

Scar reached for Mufasa's paws. He pulled his
brother close and whispered, "Long live the king!"

Then Scar let go and watched Mufasa tumble down the slope.

When the stampede was over, Simba found his father lying lifeless in the dust. "Nooo!" Simba wailed.

Scar came to the sobbing cub's side. "What have you done?" he accused.

"There were wildebeests everywhere . . . he tried to save me . . . it was an accident," Simba said. "I didn't mean to. . . ."

"Of course not. But if it weren't for you, he'd still be alive. What will your mother think?" Scar demanded.

Simba looked stricken.
"What should I do?"
"Run away," Scar advised. "Run away
and never come back."

27

Simba ran. Scar sent the hyenas after him.

The hyenas chased Simba to the border of the Pride Lands. The cub dived into a thicket of thorns at the edge of a great desert. The hyenas looked at the sharp thorns, then at the desert.

"The cub won't last a day out there," Shenzi declared.

Simba ran until he could run no more. The thirsty cub collapsed on the sand. Vultures circled him hungrily.

But Timon the meerkat and his friend, Pumbaa the warthog, found him. Simba woke up in their jungle home.

"Where are you from?" Timon asked.

Simba sighed. "It doesn't matter. I can't go back."

"What did you do, kid?" Pumbaa wondered.

"Something terrible," Simba replied.

Timon shrugged. "Who cares? You've got to put the past behind you. *Hakuna matata!*"

Timon added, "It means no worries. That's the motto we live by. And here's what we live on." Timon showed Simba a wiggly insect.

Simba watched Pumbaa eat a grub. "Slimy, but satisfying!" the warthog said with a burp.

Simba frowned, but he ate the big bug.

Then the cub smiled and said, "Hakuna matata!"

In the months that followed, Simba ate many, many
grubs and grew into a full-sized lion. Most of the time, he
was happy with his friends Timon and Pumbaa. Yet he
missed his mother and often thought of his father.

One night, as they gazed up at the stars, Simba
remembered what his father had told him. He wondered
if the great kings of the past really were looking down
from those stars. Simba felt very alone.

The next day, Simba heard Timon scream.
A hungry lioness was about to pounce on
Pumbaa, who was stuck under a log!
Timon was bravely trying to protect
him. Simba gave a mighty roar
and leapt at the lioness.

They began to fight until Simba
recognized his old friend. "Nala!" he gasped.
The lioness looked deep into the eyes of
the handsome young lion and whispered,
"Simba? Scar told us you were dead."

Nala told Simba how terrible things were now that King Scar and his hyenas ruled the Pride Lands. There was no food or water. "But you can come back and become king. Then everything will be right again," Nala said.

"I'm no king," Simba said angrily.

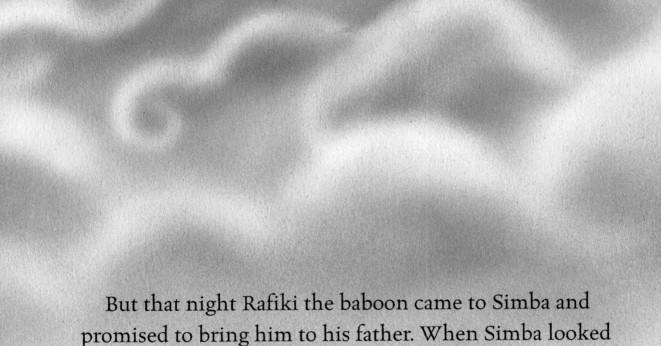

But that night Rafiki the baboon came to Simba and promised to bring him to his father. When Simba looked up at the stars, he heard a familiar voice.

"Simba," his father asked, "have you forgotten me?"

Simba gasped. "No! How could I . . ."

"You have forgotten who you are and so have forgotten me," the ghostly voice said. "Look inside yourself, Simba. You must take your place in the Circle of Life!"

Simba knew his father was right. His friends returned with him to the Pride Lands.

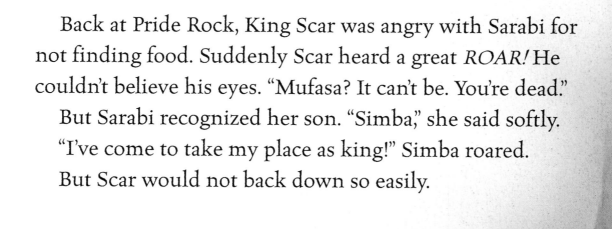

Back at Pride Rock, King Scar was angry with Sarabi for not finding food. Suddenly Scar heard a great *ROAR!* He couldn't believe his eyes. "Mufasa? It can't be. You're dead." But Sarabi recognized her son. "Simba," she said softly. "I've come to take my place as king!" Simba roared. But Scar would not back down so easily.

Simba leaped at Scar, but the villain slipped away. Instead, the hyenas rushed at Simba. Pride Rock echoed with their hideous laughter as the hyenas forced Simba to the edge of a cliff.

Scar walked up to Simba.
"Your daddy isn't here to
save you this time," Scar
taunted. Then he pushed
Simba off the cliff!

Simba's claws scrambled
for a hold on the steep slope.

"This looks familiar," Scar
sneered. "Oh, yes. It's just
the way your father looked
before I killed him."

At last, Simba knew the truth! With a mighty roar, he leapt at Scar.

Meanwhile, Timon, Pumbaa, and the lionesses had chased the hyenas off Pride Rock. Simba sent Scar flying over the cliff into the mob of hungry hyenas. Finally, they had a meal fit for a king—or a king fit for a meal!

Simba thanked his friends. Then he walked to the top of Pride Rock. His roar echoed through the Pride Lands. The rightful king had taken his throne. Simba knew that a king must have a queen. So, of course, he chose the beautiful Nala.

The plains were soon lush again, and the hunting was good once more.

Before long, the animals again came from far and near across the dusty African plain. This time, they came to greet the first-born cub of King Simba and Queen Nala.

Wise old Rafiki stood at the edge of Pride Rock and held up the cub for all to see. The elephants trumpeted and the zebras whinnied for joy as the future lion king joined the great Circle of Life.

The End

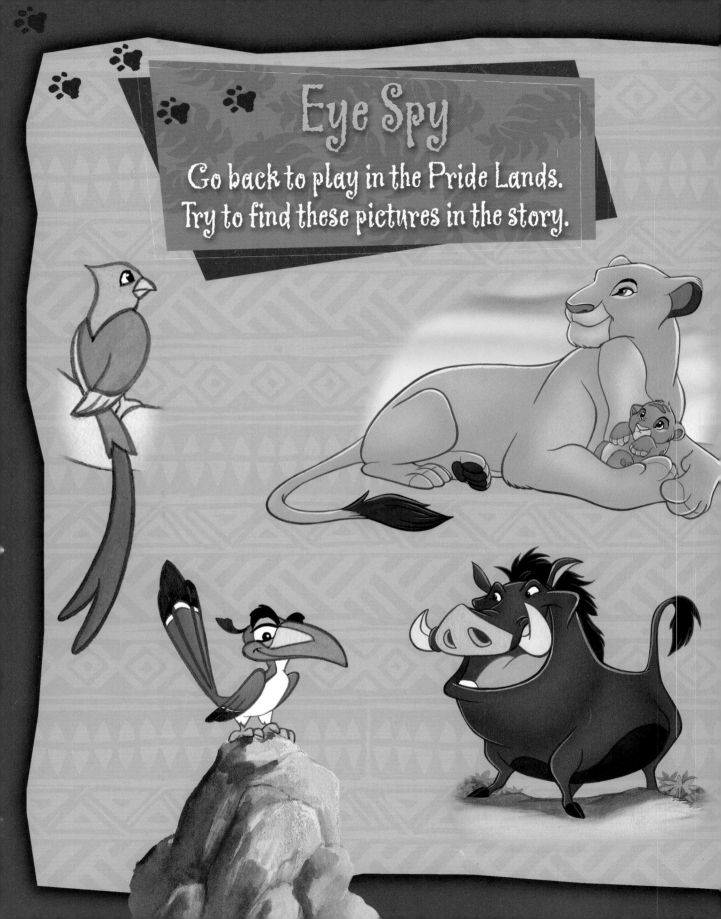

Eye Spy

Go back to play in the Pride Lands.
Try to find these pictures in the story.